DreamWorks®

HOW TO TRAIN YOUR

DRAGON

Illustrated by Colin Jack
Layouts by Art Mawhinney

Published by
Louis Weber, C.E.O., Publications International, Ltd.
7373 North Cicero Avenue, Lincolnwood, Illinois 60712

Ground Floor, 59 Gloucester Place, London W1U 8JJ

Customer Service: 1-800-595-8484 or customer_service@pilbooks.com

www.pilbooks.com

p i kids is a registered trademark of Publications International, Ltd.

Look and Find is a registered trademark of Publications International, Ltd., in the United States and in Canada.

8 7 6 5 4 3 2 1

ISBN-13: 978-1-60553-114-4 ISBN-10: 1-60553-114-6

pi
kids® publications international, ltd.

The Viking village of Berk is under attack—by dragons! The brave Vikings are doing all they can to protect their homes, but the dragons are very powerful. As the villagers wage war, be on the lookout for these different types of dragons.

This Gronkle

This Night Fury

This Deadly Nadder

This Monstrous Nightmare

This Terrible Terror

This Hideous Zippleback

Hiccup knows that being a blacksmith's apprentice is hard work. So Astrid brightens his day when she brings in her broken axe for Hiccup to fix. While Hiccup lends a hand, help him out by finding these other Viking weapons around the shop.

Spear

Shield

Bola

Sword

Mace

Axe

Stoick the Vast is every bit as huge as his name implies. But his son Hiccup is quite the opposite. Look around their dining room for these foods that might fatten up the chief's son.

Eel

Octopus

Fish

Fish tail

T-bone steak

Crab stew

Hiccup joins the other teenagers in the training ring, where they're training to battle dragons. Hiccup soon realizes it takes a lot of practice to become a good Viking. Be on the lookout for danger as you find Hiccup and his pals.

Astrid

Tuffnut

Ruffnut

Hiccup

Snotlout

Fishlegs

Hiccup's new friend Toothless, a Night Fury dragon, can fly high and fast! But no one is supposed to know they're friends. When Astrid discovers their secret, they take her for the ride of her life. As Astrid hangs on, try to spot these familiar places far below.

Training ring

Blacksmith's shop

Stoick and Hiccup's house

Meade Hall

Kids' observation tower

Toothless' cove

Uh oh! Hiccup's secret has been discovered! Gobber has found that his young Viking trainee is obsessed with dragons. Sort through the mess and find these designs that Hiccup has drawn.

Viking warrior

Dragon saddle

Dragon prosthetic tail

Mangler

Mini-mangler

Walrus

The Vikings are in deep trouble! The Red Death will surely do them in. But Hiccup and his friends have come to the rescue — with the help of some dragons! Look for the heroes as they soar through the skies.

Tuffnut

Astrid

Fishlegs

Hiccup

Ruffnut

Snotlout

The Red Death has been defeated, thanks to Hiccup and Toothless. Join the victorious Vikings as they have a good time in Meade Hall, and help them find these things that will help them celebrate.

Stein

Horn

Turkey leg

Candelabra

Goblet

Roasted pig

Hurry back to the burning town of Berk and find these valiant villagers.

Gobber

This viking

This viking

This viking

This viking

This viking

Stoick the Vast

Walk back into the blacksmith shop and look for these handy tools.

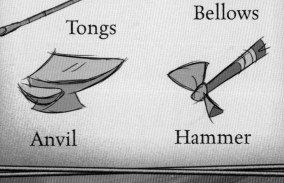

Grindstone

Extra axe head

Tongs

Bellows

Anvil

Hammer

Revisit Stoick and Hiccup's house and look for these trophies they've used to decorate it.

Sabertooth cat tusk

Caribou antlers

Bear skin

Trophy goblet

Dragon skull

Hiccup's mother's helmet

Climb back into the training ring and look for these training versions of weapons used to battle dragons.

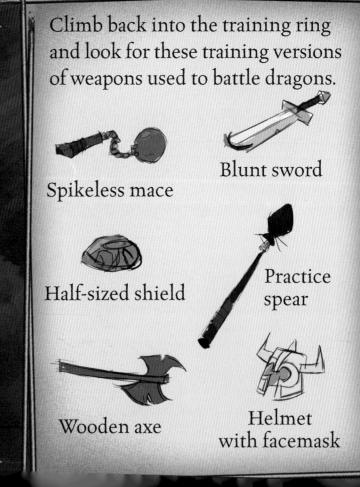

Spikeless mace

Blunt sword

Half-sized shield

Practice spear

Wooden axe

Helmet with facemask

Help Hiccup and Astrid find these stone monuments their ancestors built.

Vikinghenge

Hornhenge

Shieldhenge

Swordhenge

Serpenthenge

Dragonhenge

Go back to Gobber's blacksmith shop and find these portraits that Hiccup has drawn.

Hiccup feeding Toothless a fish

Hiccup riding Toothless

Hiccup petting Toothless

Hiccup hiding

Hiccup and his father

Hiccup winning a training battle

Fly back to the battle with the Red Death and look for these things that the dragons have stolen from the Vikings' village.

This sword

This sheep

A shield

Treasure

A sail

A golden helmet

March back into Meade Hall and find 28 dragons hidden in the tapestries, carvings, and other pieces of Viking art.